From the Porch Rocker

FROM THE PORCH ROCKER

ALI LUCE

All rights reserved. No part of this publication may be reproduced, distributed, or transmitted in any form by any means, including photocopying, recording, or other electronic methods without the prior written permission of the author, except in the case of brief quotations embodied in reviews and certain other noncommercial uses permitted by copyright law. For permission requests, write to the author at the email address below.

ali.luce.writing@gmail.com

© Ali Luce, 2024
Printed in the United States of America

ISBN: 979-8-218-38225-4

Cover illustration by Branislav Sosic
Edited by Scarlett Wills
Cover & Design by Tell Tell Poetry

First Printing, 2024

For my mom, dad, and sister, whose support in the form of huffing when I said I was a lousy writer gave me the confidence to keep going.

CONTENTS

CHAPTER ONE
Seasons

CHAPTER TWO
The Ocean

CHAPTER THREE
The Sky

CHAPTER FOUR
The Earth

CHAPTER FIVE
Friendship

ACKNOWLEDGMENTS

Firstly, I want to thank Scarlett for her exceptional editing skills and her ability to bring out the best in my writing. Without her guidance, I fear that the word "symphony" would have been used so frequently that it lost its meaning. I would also like to express my appreciation to my grandmother, whose porch rocking chair served as the catalyst for my journey into writing this collection. Furthermore, I want to extend my gratitude to Roger Wheeler State Beach, a place that has consistently offered me the perfect setting for reflection and inspiration. Last but not least, I want to express my appreciation for the White Mountains of New Hampshire for opening my eyes to new perspectives and showcasing the beauty of our world from unique vantage points. It is through exploring these breathtaking landscapes that I have gained a deeper understanding of the interconnectedness of all things. Thank you all for being instrumental in bringing this collection to life.

From the Porch Rocker

Chapter One
Seasons

FROM THE PORCH ROCKER

GRACEFULLY GOLDEN

As summer's warmth begins to wane,
a subtle shift fills the air again.
Leaves, once green, now paint a sight,
in hues of red, orange, and golden light.

They dance and swirl, a graceful glide,
floating down from trees so wide.
Like nature's confetti, a vibrant show,
Leaves falling softly, as autumns go.

They carpet the ground in a patchwork quilt,
from falling leaves, the floor is built,
Forming a path, a nostalgic embrace,
Guiding us through this fall-filled space.

With each gentle breeze that passes through,
More leaves tumble, their journey to pursue.
Whispering secrets, as they flutter and twirl,
Nature's lullaby, an autumnal swirl.

They gather in corners, hidden and deep,
Where small critters slumber, a peaceful sleep.
Providing shelter, like a cozy nest,
These fallen leaves, a gentle rest.

As the sun dips lower, and shadows grow long,
Autumn's symphony sings its song.
Leaves falling gracefully, a magical sight,
Embracing the beauty of the fading light.

ALI LUCE

In this season of change, we find our own grace,
Letting go, giving winter its space.
For though they may fall, they'll rise once more,
To start anew, a cycle to adore.

So let us embrace the autumn's call,
as leaves gently tumble and gracefully fall.
For in their journey, we find our own way,
In this ever-changing world, day by day.

FROM THE PORCH ROCKER

ORCHARD ADVENTURE

On a golden autumn's day, we set our sights,
To the orchard ripe, where joy takes flight.
Under the sun's warm glow, we wander free,
In the bountiful fields, where apples be.

With baskets in hand, we valiantly stride,
Through the red and green aisle, side by side.
The fragrance of apples dances in the air,
Whispering promises of flavors rare.

As we venture deeper, our eyes alight,
On trees adorned, a breathtaking sight.
Each branch heavy-laden with nature's delight,
Apples vibrant in hue, gleaming so bright.

We reach up high, stretching for the prize,
Collecting apples, a sweet paradise.
Their crimson skin, a lustrous sheen,
A symphony of taste, a dream serene.

With baskets overflowing and faces alight,
In the orchard's heart, we find a cozy delight.
We gather 'round the table, a candle aglow,
Drinking crisp cider, a warming show.

The aroma envelops, embracing our souls,
Cinnamon and cloves, a tale it unfolds.
As we savor the sip, a delight cascades,
Warming us inside, like autumn's serenades.

ALI LUCE

Amidst the laughter and cider's amber glow,
The memories we create, forever grow.
Friends and family, a harvest's embrace,
In the orchard's haven, a cherished space.

FROM THE PORCH ROCKER

ANTICIPATION

As autumn fades, winter draws near,
A quietly magical time of the year,
The air grows crisp, the sky turns gray,
Anticipation fills the day.

In hushed whispers, rumors spread,
Of a snowy blanket soon to be spread,
And as the days pass one by one,
We yearn for flakes beneath the sun.

Then on a morning, cold and bright,
A wondrous sight greets our delight,
Softly falling from the sky above,
The first snowflake, a symbol of love.

Dancing, twirling, through the air,
Creating a landscape calm and fair,
Each delicate flake, a work of art,
Gracefully painting the world in white.

Children's laughter fills the air,
As they build snowmen without a care,
Their footprints leaving trails behind,
As they make angels, hearts entwined.

The trees, once bare, now wear a crown,
Of snowy jewels that cascade down,
Branches heavy, glistening bright,
A stunning sight, a winter's delight.

ALI LUCE

Footsteps muffled, silence makes,
As snowflakes kiss the ground, it takes,
A magical silence, oh so pure,
A hushed calmness we can't ignore.

By flickering fire, we gather near,
With loved ones, friends, we hold so dear,
Drinking cocoa, warmth in each sip,
As we watch the snowfall, soft and crisp.

The first snow of the winter season,
A symbol of hope, a simple reason,
To marvel at nature's sublime art,
And find joy in a snowflake's start.

FROM THE PORCH ROCKER

WINTER'S CHILL

In the chill of winter's grasp, we huddle near the fire,
Embraced by warmth's sweetest caress, our souls begin to inspire.
A concert of crackling flame, a dance of glowing sparks,
We bundle up like cozy cats, as cold outside remarks.

The air is crisp and biting, a wintry force we bear,
But within our cozy haven, we find solace and repair.
Wrapped in our scarves and woolen coats, our bodies snug and tight,
We sip hot cocoa by the blaze, a comforting delight.

As frost paints patterns on windows, like nature's work of art,
We revel in serenity that heats both mind and heart.
Blankets piled high upon us, like clouds on a chilly night,
We gather near the fireplace, its flickering, golden light.

The crackling logs whisper tales, as embers dance with mirth,
And within this harmonious scene, we find our souls rebirthed.
The world outside may freeze and bite, entangled in a chill,
But inside by the glowing hearth, all worries they stand still.

A chorus of comfort, the fire's warm embrace,
With every toasty breath we take, a sigh of frozen grace.
Together, we weave memories, in this haven we create,
Where chilly weather's icy touch slows down its frantic gait.

Though clouds loom dark, and cold winds blow,
Winter has its own beautiful flow,
Blanketing the world in a serene chill,
A perfect backdrop for winter's thrill.

ALI LUCE

So, bundle up, dear friends, by the fire's gentle hymn,
As winter's chill may weave its tale, our spirits it can't dim.
For in these moments, warm and bright, by the heat we conspire,
To love and cherish the life that blooms, while bundled by the fire.

FROM THE PORCH ROCKER

REAWAKENING

In spring's embrace, the flowers awaken,
From their slumber, by winter forsaken,
Petals unfurl, like a vibrant display,
Blossoming hues celebrate the day.

Dainty daffodils, with golden grace,
Sway in the wind, elegantly embrace,
Their buttery glow, a radiant light,
Enchanting all, with their cheerful delight.

Tulips emerge, in a rainbow of shades,
Bold and beautiful, like color cascades,
Crimson, pink, and lilac, they yawn and cry,
An array of petals, reaching for the sky.

Cherry blossoms, delicate and fair,
Fragile petals dance in the air,
A blush of pink, adorning every tree,
Whispering secrets of love's sweet decree.

Lily of the valley, in white attire,
Fragrance so sweet, it sets hearts on fire,
Delightfully tickling the senses and nose,
As their fragrant aroma ebbs and flows.

The violet flaunts a purple crown,
Peeking from the ground to the world renowned,
Whispering promises of dreams come true,
With petals so soft, like morning dew.

ALI LUCE

As nature awakens and springs to life,
The flowers bloom, erasing winter's strife,
A harmony of colors, a sight to behold,
In spring's tender touch, a story untold.

FROM THE PORCH ROCKER

A NECESSARY PLIGHT

April Showers bring May Flowers,
A phenomenon that enchants for hours.
As raindrops dance and gently fall,
They nourish the Earth, one and all.

The skies are gray, the clouds so dreary,
But in this gloom, a promise so cheery.
For with each raindrop that softly lands,
Nature's beauty begins to expand.

The flowers lay asleep beneath the ground,
Awaiting their chance to astound.
With every shower, their patience bloomed,
As Mother Nature's masterpiece is resumed.

Lush green leaves upon the trees,
An emerald canopy sways in the breeze.
Blossoms and buds burst forth in delight,
Stealing hearts with colors so bright.

April showers are but a necessary plight,
For they bring forth nature's purest delight.
May flowers, a beauty of old,
Soothes all souls, as nature unfolds.

ALI LUCE

SUNLIGHT THROUGH THE FENCE

Under a summer sunset sky,
On the porch, tranquility lies.
The sun bids the world adieu,
Painting the heavens in hues so true.

An artist's palette of orange and pink,
Cast upon the sky's fragile brink.
The sun sinks lower, closer to rest,
As the colors dance upon nature's crest.

The chirping birds softly sing,
A sweet melody that gently rings.
The flowers bloom with vibrant grace,
As twilight's kisses gently embrace.

A warm breeze whispers through the air,
Caressing each strand of my hair.
The potted flowers swing to and fro,
As the evening's melody begins to grow.

A chorus of crickets fills the night,
As the stars twinkle with pure delight.
Fireflies dance in their own ballet,
Lighting up the summer's way.

The scent of blossoms fills my lungs,
As nature's lullaby is softly sung.
On the porch, I find my solace,
As the day fades with graceful promise.

FROM THE PORCH ROCKER

In this moment, time stands still,
A summer's sunset, a tranquil thrill.
The porch becomes my sacred shrine,
As I bask in this evening divine.

ALI LUCE

BAREFOOT

In the summer heat, I find delight,
As I wander barefoot under the sunlight.
Free from the confines of shoes on my feet,
I tread upon Mother Earth, an intimate retreat.

With every step, sand tickles my toes,
As I roam along the seashore's rolls.
The ocean breeze sings a song divine,
Guiding me on a path where treasures shine.

Golden grains dance under my soles,
As the sun kisses my skin in radiant folds.
I follow the trail that nature provides,
Through wildflowers and grassy tides.

Leaves whisper beneath my gentle tread,
As I stroll through a forest, wide and spread.
Cool dewdrops greet me in meadows, lush and fair,
Where cares dissolve into the fragrant air.

Barefoot I wander, feeling every sensation,
Connected to Earth's powerful vibration.
From green meadows to rocky landscapes bold,
I traverse nature's wonders, untamed and untold.

The warmth of the ground embraces my feet,
While tranquility and bliss become complete.
I revel in the simple joy this moment brings,
As barefoot, through summer's beauty, my soul takes wings.

Chapter Two
The Ocean

FROM THE PORCH ROCKER

DISTANT SHORES

Oh, behold the rhythmic roar
Of waves crashing upon the shore.
A masterpiece of nature's might
In the darkness of the night.

With thunderous force they swiftly break,
Their mighty power leaves hearts to shake.
A dance of foam and salty spray,
Whispering tales of a distant bay.

Like a painter's brush on canvas white,
They sweep the sand with all their might.
Creating art in the sandy bed,
As shells and seaweed are gently spread.

Each wave eager to reach the land,
Like a determined soldier taking its stand.
Cresting high with graceful pride,
Then, crashing down, a thrilling ride.

The seagulls sing their joyful hymn,
As the waves keep rolling in a rhythmic trim
An orchestra of crashing sound
Echoes through the coast, all around.

They carry secrets from distant lands,
And leave treasures in their foamy hands.
From distant shores and deep blue seas
They bring memories to those who plead.

So, come and embrace this natural show,
As the waves crash and mighty forces flow
Let the melody of their crashing sound
Paint a masterpiece that will astound.

FROM THE PORCH ROCKER

WATERY TIDE

I sail upon the ocean wide,
Where waters dance and waves collide.
With the wind as my faithful guide,
I journey on this rocking ride.

The salty breeze caresses my face,
As sea foam dances with gentle grace.
Whispering secrets, it leaves no trace,
A melody of waves in its embrace.

The sun reflects upon deep blue,
Sparkling like diamonds, a mesmerizing view.
Where horizons call, I'm drawn to pursue,
Uncharted territories, to venture anew.

In solitude, I find solace profound,
No city's chaos or crowded ground.
Just the rhythmic sound, of waves around,
A tranquil haven, where freedom is found.

Oh, the tales these waves could tell,
Of ancient legends where sirens dwell.
With courage, against tempests we rebel,
Undeterred by storms, the maritime spell.

In each sunrise and sunset divine,
The ocean's beauty forever will shine.
A canvas painted by the earth's own design,
A precious gift, for hearts to intertwine.

ALI LUCE

So, let us sail on the ocean wide,
Where dreams and destinies coincide.
A sailor's heart, forever untied,
To find adventure on this watery tide.

FROM THE PORCH ROCKER

PAGES ON THE SEA

Beside the shore where waves crash and roar,
I find solace in books at the seashore.
Beneath the sun's warm, golden embrace,
I lose myself in tales of another place.

A world of wonder rests in each page,
As I escape the present, like a sage.
The sand tickles my toes, the breeze whispers in my ear,
and I am transported to realms where dreams appear.

Characters become friends, their stories a delight,
As I sit on my towel, reading till twilight.
Words dance before me, bringing scenes to life,
A chorus of imagination, away from daily strife.

The rhythm of the waves orchestrates my mind,
As I immerse myself, leaving reality behind.
The saltwater spray refreshes my soul,
Enchanting me, making me whole.

The books transport me to a place serene,
Where the only sound is the ocean's keen.
The scent of sea air fills my lungs, my heart,
Inspiring me to explore, to create my own art.

Thus, I spend my days by the beach, reading away,
Eyes glued to the words, no time to stray.
Lost in a world where possibilities abound,
Reading at the beach, my peace is found.

ALI LUCE

SEASHELLS

On a sandy stretch by the soothing sea,
I embarked on a wondrous quest with glee.
Searching, seeking, with eager eyes,
For treasures amidst the seagull cries.

Beneath the cerulean sky's embrace,
I longed to discover shells' delicate grace.
Their myriad colors and shapes unknown,
Tales of their journey, carefully sown.

Weaving through the waves, with nimble feet,
I combed the shore, my senses complete.
Each shell I found, a pearl of the shore,
Whispering secrets that we tend to ignore.

The scallops, with patterns like flaming sunsets,
Astonished me, like art one never forgets.
The periwinkles, shining in pearlescent glow,
Carried whispers of love from long ago.

Amongst the jingle shells, at the ocean's edge,
I found wisdom waiting to be dredged.
Expressing stories of tides and renewal,
They reminded me of life's constant duel.

And as the waves gently kissed my bare feet,
I marveled at nature's rhythm, so sweet.
For every shell carried a story of its own,
A sliver of history, forever unknown.

FROM THE PORCH ROCKER

In this search for shells, I found much more,
Appreciation, wonder, a deeply felt rapport.
A connection with nature, a bond so pure,
Amidst the seashells, memories endure.

So, if ever you wander along the shore,
Remember to never overlook the shells' lore.
For amidst their beauty lies stories untold,
Whispered by the ocean, eternal and bold.

ALI LUCE

JELLYFISH

In the depth of the ocean's sway,
Where the mysteries of the sea hold sway,
There floats a creature both delicate and grand,
With a glowing crown and a soothing hand.

Its name is whispered in awe and hush,
The graceful dweller, the jellyfish gush,
With tentacles waving, like ribbons unfurled,
It dances and glides, in a watery world.

Its body translucent, like a moonbeam's glow,
It radiates beauty, as the currents flow,
With colors so vibrant, a kaleidoscope sight,
It enchants all who witness its ethereal light.

Beneath the moon's reflection, it starts to rise,
Floating with serenity, and love in its eyes,
Through the ebb and flow, it drifts and sways,
Guided by the rhythm of the ocean's embrace.

Yet, beware the tentacles that hang below,
For though it may grace, they can sting and bestow,
A gentle touch can bring a whisper of pain,
A reminder of the wildness that lies within its domain.

Its presence, a reminder of nature's art,
Of ancient wonders that capture the heart,
For in this vast world where creatures abound,
The jellyfish reigns, in silent beauty profound.

FROM THE PORCH ROCKER

FOOTPRINTS

As I stroll upon the sandy shore,
The tranquil waves crash and roar,
The glistening sun kisses my face,
Walking on this beach, my heart begins to race.

Beneath my feet, the soft grains shift,
Leaving footprints, a personal gift,
The salty breeze brushes through my hair,
A feeling of freedom, beyond compare.

Seagulls soar in the endless sky,
Their calls of joy, echoing high,
I walk along and collect seashells,
Each a memory, each a story to tell.

The rhythmic tides cleanse my soul,
Leaving behind worries that once took a toll,
The lapping water erases all strife,
Walking on this beach is the cure to life.

Sandcastles rise with childish delight,
Children's laughter fills air, so bright,
Grinning, I splash through the foamy tide,
Pure bliss in every step, by the ocean's side.

As the sun dips beyond the horizon's edge,
Colors explode, leaving me on a ledge,
A peacefulness settles within my core,
Walking on this beach, I am forever restored.

ALI LUCE

With the moon's soft glow guiding my way,
I continue wandering, without delay,
The whispers of seashells, secrets they share,
Walking on the beach, a moment so rare.

On this shore, dreams come alive,
And worries vanish as the waves strive,
Walking on this beach, I feel complete,
In nature's embrace, finding emotions so sweet.

With every step, I let go of strife,
Finding harmony in the rhythm of life,
Walking on the beach, a timeless dance,
Where nature and soul find their true chance.

FROM THE PORCH ROCKER

SHORELINE

Upon the sandy shore I stand,
Where land and sea collide and blend,
I find a peace that's hard to ignore,
As the sun's gentle rays begin to pour.

The waves crash in a steady dance,
As seagulls soar and waves advance,
The salty air upon my face,
Carries me to a tranquil place.

The turquoise waters stretch so wide,
Inviting me to take a stride,
With each step, the sand beneath my feet,
Resurfaces memories bittersweet.

A mesmerizing sight to see,
The ebb and flow, so wild and free,
With every wave that sweeps ashore,
Washing away all troubles I bore.

The ocean's voice I hear,
Welcomes all, far and near,
As shells and pebbles caress my toes,
I feel a sense of calm repose.

The sun above, a golden hue,
Paints the sky with colors anew,
Reflecting off the waters vast,
Mirroring the beauty unsurpassed.

ALI LUCE

The glistening, endless horizon,
Fills my soul with tranquil passion,
In this timeless, sacred space,
Earth's wonders I embrace.

And as the sun begins to set,
Casting a golden fiery net,
I bid farewell to the ocean's shore,
But in my heart, it lingers evermore.

Chapter Three
The Sky

FROM THE PORCH ROCKER

CLEAR BLUE

In a world full of wonder, I raise my eyes high,
To the heavens above, where dreams seem to fly.
Oh, what a sight, a canvas so vast,
A clear blue sky, holding moments that last.

As it stretches beyond, in hues so serene,
The sky tells tales like a celestial queen.
With brush strokes of cobalt, it paints portraits rare,
A masterpiece of peace, suspended in the air.

The sun's golden fire ignites a symphony,
As rays dance and shimmer, setting spirits free.
The warmth it bestows, a comforting embrace,
A gentle reminder of life's endless grace.

The clouds, they meander, fluffy and light,
Drifting like feathers through the day and the night.
They form shapes and stories, for us to explore,
A floating art gallery, forever adored.

The birds, oh how they spread their wings wide,
Gliding through the sky, in a graceful stride.
Their melodious chorus, a song of harmony,
A sweet melody, carried by the breeze.

With each passing moment, the sky unfolds,
A captivating tale, never to be told.
It whispers secrets, as it watches us below,
A tapestry of wonders, forever on show.

ALI LUCE

So, let us gaze up, with hearts full of delight,
To the boundless beauty, that fills our sight.
For in this clear blue sky, we find solace and peace,
A reminder that life's joys will never cease.

FROM THE PORCH ROCKER

DANCING CLOUDS

Beneath the endless blue expanse,
I lie upon the grass's dance,
With clouds like cotton, soft and white,
Like fleeting dreams in gentle flight.

I watch them shape and shift with ease,
Creating stories in the breeze,
A lion's mane, a rabbit's ear,
A pirate ship that's full of cheer.

They drift in patterns ever grand,
Like nature's brush upon the land,
A swirling canvas in the sky,
Where art and visions intertwine.

I find serenity way up high,
Where clouded thoughts seem to comply,
With peaceful moments, free from strife,
A respite from the rush of life.

I marvel at their sheer display,
and how they can change from day to day,
From wispy trails to billows bold,
Each formation a tale untold.

And as they pass, so too I find,
A sense of calm within my mind,
For cloud watching, it seems to be,
A mindful exercise for me.

ALI LUCE

So here I lie, with open heart,
In awe of nature's stunning art,
Lost in the vastness of the view,
Embracing clouds, my soul anew.

FROM THE PORCH ROCKER

DARKER SKIES

In the realm of colors, a muted hue,
A shade of solemnity, calm and true.
Above us stretches, so vast and high,
The canvas of nature, the blue-grey sky.

With clouds like whispers, they dance and twirl,
As if painting the sky with a mystical swirl.
Their gentle movements, so light and free,
Unleashing a story for us to see.

Sometimes, it weeps, shedding tears of rain,
Cleansing the Earth, relieving its pain.
Each drop a rhythm, a melodious sound,
Falling from above, to the thirsty ground.

The grey sky holds secrets untold,
Stories of mysteries, waiting to unfold.
It wraps us in stillness, a sense of calm,
As we contemplate life's infinite charm.

In its serenity, it offers a chance,
To ponder and dream, to take a stance.
To reflect upon moments, both past and new,
Under the veils of grey, where dreams come true.

ALI LUCE

CELESTIAL WONDERS

Stars twinkle, scattered across dark blue,
As the night sky unveils its celestial view.
Moon beams softly grace the canvas above,
Creating a magical tapestry we can't get enough of.

Constellations form exquisite works of art,
Connecting dots that tell stories from the start.
Orion the hunter, his belt shining so bright,
Guiding lost souls through the vastness of night.

The Milky Way stretches like a silvery stream,
A cosmic river where dreams are set free.
Planets waltz in their celestial dance,
Each one a mystery, in the starry expanse.

Saturn flaunts its majestic ringed attire,
Jupiter radiates its fiery desire.
Mars proudly displays its vibrant red hue,
Venus twinkles, casting enchantment anew.

As darkness descends and the night sky awakens,
Old tales and folklore become unshaken.
Whispers of ancient gods and distant lands,
Echo through the heavens, crafted by unseen hands.

Shooting stars streak across the night sky without a trace,
Granting wishes through time and endless space.
While comets blaze with a celestial flair,
Reminding us of the wonders that exist up there.

FROM THE PORCH ROCKER

The night sky, a cosmic masterpiece on display,
A collection of stardust, leading the way.
Captivating our souls, igniting our dreams,
Forever mesmerizing with its celestial gleams.

So let us gaze up, in awe and contemplation,
Embracing the beauty of this cosmic creation.
For the night sky, a celestial source of delight,
A reminder of the wonders that reside in the night.

ALI LUCE

STARRY SERENADE

Starry serenade, a lullaby divine,
Underneath the constellations we recline.
Contentment fills the air, as we lay low,
In the backyard grass where warm breezes blow.

Midsummer night, a tapestry of dreams,
Where stars paint stories in celestial streams.
Their twinkling lights, like words on a page,
Tell a story, of a different age.

The moon's gentle glow casts a magic spell,
As we soak up the peace that it expels.
Whispers of love, carried across the sky,
In this cosmic sanctuary, oh so high.

Pegasus gallops among shimmering specks,
While Orion guards with his mighty flex.
The Big Dipper points to our heart's desire,
Guiding us through this celestial choir.

A moment of wonder, tranquil and still,
As time stands suspended on this earthly hill.
We bask in the beauty of this starlit show,
Grateful for the magnificence that it bestows.

Stargazing delight, your enchantment immense,
Filling our souls with love, so intense.
In nature's embrace, we find our retreat,
Beneath the velvet sky, serene and sweet.

FROM THE PORCH ROCKER

SUNRISE HAZE

In the dawn's golden haze, on a bench I reside,
Dew-kissed grass beneath me, a moment to bide.
The sky blushes softly as the night takes its leave,
And the clouds dance above, soothing patterns they weave.

Twinkling stars bid farewell, as daylight breaks through,
Painting hues of enchantment upon the vast blue.
A canvas full of colors, a palette divine,
As the sun stretches its rays, making shadows recline.

The world awakens in this magical hour,
Birds joining in chorus from tree and from bower.
A zephyr whispers among the tall trees,
As nature harmonizes, carried by morning breeze.

Clouds drift like cotton candy, floating up high,
Their shapes taking form amidst the tranquil sky.
Bunnies and dragons playfully come into view,
Creating dreamscape wonders for me and for you.

A feeling of wonder envelops my soul,
As nature's own lullaby takes its sweet toll.
Joy and serenity blend into one,
Watching as daybreak unfolds with the sun.

So let us sit together on this peaceful morn,
And witness this spectacle that was duly born.
In awe of nature's canvas, let our hearts rejoice,
As we find solace in the melody of morning's voice.

ALI LUCE

AN ECLIPSE'S GLORIOUS TALE

In the vast expanse of the sky above,
A wondrous event begins to unfold.
An eclipse, with its captivating hue,
Casts a shadow, both mysterious and bold.

Don't dare stare directly at its face,
For its beauty renders human eyes blind.
But fear not, for its grandeur we embrace,
A spectacle that warms our hearts and mind.

As the sun retreats behind the moon's cloak,
The sky darkens, a celestial dance.
Stars twinkle brightly, an ethereal stroke,
In this cosmic theater, we have a chance.

To witness the union of light and shade,
Nature painting the celestial dome.
A sight that leaves us utterly amazed,
As in harmony, sun and moon find their home.

The moon wears an ebony mask with pride,
Eclipsing the radiance of solar rays.
Mankind looks up with wonder worldwide,
Lost within nature's enigmatic ways.

We ponder the great mysteries it unveils,
The interconnectedness of all that is bright.
Through shadowed moments, our curiosity sails,
Exploring unknown realms in sheer delight.

FROM THE PORCH ROCKER

And as the eclipse gracefully moves along,
Returning light to a world held in awe.
Our souls are touched by this special song,
Forever remembering what we saw.

Chapter Four

The Earth

FROM THE PORCH ROCKER

HOMELY PLANET

O Earth, forgiving home of blue and green,
A precious gem amid the cosmic scene.
Your fertile lands, where life so beautifully thrives,
Where nature sings and dances, truly alive.

From soaring mountaintops to oceans deep,
Your boundless wonders, secrets to keep.
In forests tall, a tapestry of green,
A sanctuary where serenity is seen.

Your rivers flow, a gentle lullaby,
Through valleys and canyons, they glide and fly.
They nourish life with crystal-clear grace,
A lifeline for creatures, in every place.

Beneath your soil, a world unseen,
Where roots embrace, and life convenes.
From tiny insects to the mighty trees,
A cluster of life in perfect glee.

But alas, dear Earth, we must take heed,
For our actions sow the seeds of greed.
With reckless hands, we harm and destroy,
Our thoughtless actions, a painful ploy.

Let us unite, and heal your wounds,
Preserve your treasures, reverse the tunes.
For in your care, we find our hope,
To cherish you, Earth, we must learn to cope.

ALI LUCE

For you are more than just a home,
A sacred place, where life does roam.
Let us be stewards of the land we tread,
Protecting your splendor, a common thread.

O Earth, our fragile and resilient friend,
May we mend the broken and learn to tend.
For in your embrace, we find our worth,
In awe of your beauty, precious Earth.

FROM THE PORCH ROCKER

MOTHER NATURE

In the realm of nature's might,
Mother Earth, a wondrous sight,
She birthed mountains tall and wide,
And oceans vast, where creatures hide.

From forests green to deserts dry,
She paints landscapes beneath the sky,
With gentle touch, she breathes and weaves,
A world of wonder that never leaves.

Her rivers, like veins, unfurl and flow,
Nourishing life wherever they go,
From babbling brooks to roaring falls,
Her water sings, her power calls.

From the smallest seed to ancient trees,
Mother Nature sets creatures free,
She nurtures life in every form,
As gentle breezes whisper, a soothing storm.

Birds take flight with melodies sweet,
Creatures roam on nimble feet,
Through her care, they live with mirth,
For Mother Nature nurtures the Earth.

Let's cherish her, this precious land,
With gratitude and gentle hand,
Protect her beauty, her sacred fire,
For with her grace, we can't deny her.

ALI LUCE

ODE TO GRASS STAINS

Oh, grass stains on my clothing, a mark of my play,
A reminder of endless hours spent outdoors all day.
In fields and in gardens, I freely did roam,
Leaving my garments with earthy stains to be shown.

From careless tumbles and spirited races across the lawn,
These vivid green marks tell tales of joyful moments gone.
As I ventured through meadows, my cares cast away,
The grass became my playground, where I'd laugh, jump, and sway.

Each stain upon my clothing portrays a cherished scene,
Where I danced with nature, carefree and serene.
In barefooted delight, I would twirl and flutter,
Smudging my clothes with nature's vibrant color.

From picnics under trees, with laughter filling the air,
To rolling down hills without a single care,
The grass stains became badges of honor and delight,
Symbolizing memories that forever stay bright.

Though some may fault my attire for being in disarray,
I see beauty in these stains, as they whisper and say,
"Remember those days of youthful glee,
When you reveled in nature, wild and free."

So let the grass stains adorn my clothes with pride,
As reminders of joyful memories that abide.
For in each vibrant mark, a story is told,
Of a life well-lived and adventures yet to unfold.

FROM THE PORCH ROCKER

ROCKS, BUGS, AND HAPPY HEARTS

In the garden green, where wonders thrive,
A child's delight, where dreams come alive,
With nimble fingers, and curious eyes,
Finding rocks and bugs, what a grand surprise!

In the dirt we dig, with joyful delight,
Unearthing mysteries hidden from sight,
Tiny creatures scuttle, beneath the ground,
While shiny pebbles in the sun are found.

A ladybug dressed in a coat of red,
Lands on a hand, a friendship widespread,
Its tiny wings flutter, oh so free,
A cherished companion, for all to see.

With dirt-stained hands, and grins so wide,
We explore nature's treasures, side by side,
Spiderwebs glistening, like threads of lace,
Weaving stories of this enchanted place.

Frogs hop along, on lily pads they dance,
As we chase butterflies, in a playful trance,
Every step we take, a new surprise we find,
Truly, in this world, no moment is confined.

With rocks like mountains, we aim to build,
A fortress of imagination, untamed and skilled,
Through paths of mud, our feet shall tread,
As we create kingdoms, inside our heads.

ALI LUCE

So let us run, and embrace the earth's delights,
Discovering joy in the simplest of sights,
For in finding rocks and bugs, and playing with dirt,
We find a world of magic, hidden, not overt.

FROM THE PORCH ROCKER

A DANCE IN THE RAIN

In the wilderness, where dreams are found,
There lies a whimsical, magical ground.
With skies draped in shades of blue and grey,
And gentle drops of rain that find their way.

The desire to join this wondrous dance
Echoes through every timid glance.
But fear holds tight, a grip too strong,
Afraid of getting wet, it seems so wrong.

Yet, dear child, hear this with an open heart,
The rain is nature's way to gently impart,
A cleansing touch upon your very soul,
To wash away worries and make you whole.

For Mother Nature whispers secrets, wise and true,
In every droplet shimmering like morning dew.
She reminds us to shed our inhibitions away,
To embrace the rain and seize the day.

So, don your boots and grab an umbrella too,
Step outside and let the raindrops fall on you.
Feel the rhythm as they patter on your skin,
A tender pattern that invites you in.

There's magic waiting in every single drop,
A chance for you to dance and surely never stop.
Release your fears, relinquish all your doubt,
And let the rain cleanse everything inside out.

ALI LUCE

As each puddle becomes a mirror reflecting delight,
You'll discover a world where everything feels right.
In this enchanting world of rain and cloud,
You'll find beauty, without a doubt.

So run through the storm with joy-filled glee,
Let the raindrops cleanse you, wild and free.
For in this dance of nature's sweetest refrain,
You'll find pure bliss—a moment that will sustain.

FROM THE PORCH ROCKER

THE GARDEN'S BOUNTY

Upon the fertile earth I kneel,
With trowel in hand, and heart filled with zeal.
In nature's loving embrace, I delve,
To sow the seeds of life, I'm compelled.

Tomatoes red as sunsets bold,
Basil fragrant, a treasure of gold.
Cucumbers crisp and cool as dew,
Carrots vibrant in shades of orange hue.

Mother Nature grants her endless wealth,
Her gentle touch enhances the health
Of growth and beauty in this sacred ground,
A sanctuary where life is found.

With tender care, I tend each sprout,
Nourishing their spirits without a doubt.
They reach for sunlight, skyward they climb,
For warmth and light, they doth entwine.

Insects dance upon each sturdy stem,
Pollinating blossoms, a vital gem.
Butterflies flutter and bees buzz with glee,
A display of life for all to see.

As days pass by in the warmth of the sun,
The garden flourishes, its bounty begun.
The vines entangle, the foliage spreads wide,
Nature's artwork painted with great pride.

ALI LUCE

We reap what we sow from this earthly art,
Cherishing every bite from nature's heart.
For she provides abundantly without end,
A reminder of her love she does send.

So let us tend to this garden fair,
With gratitude for gifts beyond compare.
In Mother Nature's embrace we reside,
Her endless wonders filling us with pride.

Chapter Five
Friendship

FROM THE PORCH ROCKER

THE TRUEST FRIENDS

In friendships true, a bond we find,
A treasure rare, so hard to bind.
Through thick and thin, they're by our side,
With love and laughter, they easily glide.

Like stars that twinkle, bright and clear,
They bring us light when shadows near.
Through tear-stained trials and joyful glee,
Best friends are there eternally.

They know our flaws, but love us still,
No judgment harsh, their hearts do fill.
With gentle words and open ears,
They soothe our doubts and calm our fears.

Through whispered secrets and shared dreams,
Best friends stand strong, a steady team.
Their loyalty unwavering, constant and true,
In stormy weather, they'll see us through.

With endless banter and playful jest,
They bring us joy when we're distressed.
In laughter's embrace, we're made complete,
Best friends make life so incredibly sweet.

Like blooms that blossom in spring's embrace,
Best friends add color to life's vast space.
They lift us up when we're feeling low,
With friendship's power, they help us grow.

ALI LUCE

Through trials faced and battles won,
Best friends are there, with the rising sun.
They celebrate our victories grand,
And lend a shoulder, when we need a hand.

FROM THE PORCH ROCKER

OUR SHIELDS

In the summer sun, our laughter soars,
As we gather to play with friends galore.
With sticks in hand, we chase dreams and goals,
Creating memories that warm our souls.

On the green grass, we form a team,
United by laughter, like a beautiful dream.
We dribble the ball, with nimble feet,
Celebrating victories, oh so sweet.

In the playground, we let our spirits soar,
Climbing, swinging, seeking adventures and more.
With fearless hearts, we conquer the heights,
Savoring the thrill, like fearless knights.

Through days and nights, we never tire,
Building castles of sand, higher and higher.
With buckets and shovels, we sculpt and shape,
A masterpiece of fun, we proudly make.

In the backyard, we run wild and free,
Playing games of tag, our energy we release.
Chasing shadows, like the wind in our hair,
Laughter echoing through the summer air.

In the park, we race against the breeze,
Balancing on ropes, with grace and ease.
Together we swing, to the highest peak,
Feeling the rush as we reach for the sky, no longer meek.

ALI LUCE

In the pool, we splash and play,
Creating ripples, like a musical display.
In water fights fierce, we find pure joy,
Diving deep, like dolphins in search of a toy.

As the sun sets, painting the sky in gold,
We gather once more, our stories unfold.
In the precious moments we all hold dear,
Friendship becomes our shield, void of fear.

Playing with friends, our hearts entwined,
The world becomes magical, one of a kind.
Through laughter and joy, we find delight,
These moments with friends shine ever so bright.

FROM THE PORCH ROCKER

A FRIEND'S EMBRACE

In times of need, when troubles abound,
There's a remedy that can be found.
A simple gesture, yet it holds so dear,
A hug from a friend, a balm to the fear.

When skies are dark, and spirits are low,
A friend's embrace can make worries go.
Arms entwined, a connection so strong,
In that warm embrace, we feel we belong.

A hug from a friend, it carries so much,
A healing touch, a gentle clutch.
It speaks of love that words can't express,
A comforting gesture, to ease distress.

In that embrace, there's no need for words,
A hug from a friend transcends all hurts.
It says, "I'm here, I understand,
Lean on me, for I'll lend a hand."

When tears are falling, and smiles are scarce,
A friend's hug proves we're not alone in these despairs.
Their arms encircle, like a protective shield,
Offering solace, helping wounds to be healed.

So, cherish those hugs, they hold magic untold,
For in those moments, friendships unfold.
A hug from a friend, a stroke of the hair,
A reminder that someone truly does care.

ALI LUCE

LAUGHING AMONGST WAVES

In the golden sands, where the waves gently roll,
Laughter fills the air, like a harmonious stroll.
Friends gathered together, a joyous band,
Sharing tales and jokes, hand in hand.

The sun shines bright, casting its warm embrace,
As we bask in the delight of this blissful space.
With each giggle and chuckle, troubles wash away,
On this sandy canvas, in perfect display.

The waves crash with glee, joining in the fun,
As our laughter carries, echoing under the sun.
We skip and we dance, like carefree children at play,
In this seaside paradise, where happiness holds sway.

The salty breeze whispers secrets in our ear,
As we revel in moments, so precious and clear.
With every comical tale, a new memory is born,
In this laughter-filled haven, where friendships adorn.

Time drifts by, like the tides that ebb and flow,
But our bond grows stronger, wherever we may go.
For in this laughter on the beach, we find solace and peace,
A testament to friendships that never cease.

FROM THE PORCH ROCKER

THE NERVOUS ADVENTURE

In a world of whispers and laughter,
Where friendships are born,
I venture, with butterflies swirling,
Into new realms, feeling quite forlorn.

A playground, bustling with joy,
Children playing without a care,
But my heart, it fluttered and danced,
As I sought someone to share.

Around me they twirled and spun,
In games of tag and chase,
Yet I stood frozen, feeling small,
Lost amidst the race.

With trembling hands I reached for courage,
And took a tentative step ahead,
Hoping to find a companion,
To comfort my fears and dread.

And then I glimpsed a friendly smile,
A beacon of hope amidst the crowd,
I approached with hesitation,
But I knew I had to stand proud.

We exchanged shy glances at first,
Like birds in a brand-new nest,
But soon our giggles filled the air
As we embarked on this quest.

ALI LUCE

Through secret hideouts in make-believe lands,
We explored the world anew.
Together we laughed, together we soared,
This friendship felt pure and true.

No longer were we two strangers lost
In an overwhelming sea.
Bound by the thread of newfound trust,
We blossomed like flowers wild and free.

The nerves that once held me captive,
Now gave way to boundless glee.
For in the heart of a new friendship,
I discovered what it means to truly be.

So let us embrace those nervous moments,
And step into the unknown with might.
For if we tread bravely through uncharted paths,
We may find a friend who brings us pure delight.

FROM THE PORCH ROCKER

THE DRIFTING FRIENDS

Once close, now drifting apart,
Friends that once held one another's heart.
A sadness lingers in the air,
As distance grows, we cannot repair.

It's natural, they say, for bonds to change,
And it doesn't mean we are to blame.
Time moves on, and paths diverge,
Leaving us feeling a bittersweet surge.

The memories we shared still stay,
Though slowly fading with each passing day.
The laughter and tears, the stories we told,
Now distant echoes as friendships unfold.

It's scary, indeed, to face the unknown,
To find new allies when we feel alone.
But deep within, a strength resides,
Courage to seek companions by our sides.

Friends may drift away like waves at sea,
Yet new ones can bloom like flowers so free.
The world is vast, with hearts yet met,
Opportunities to embrace and beget.

So let us cherish the friends of old,
For the lessons learned and stories all told.
Embrace the change and let it teach,
That life is a journey within reach.

ALI LUCE

The drifting friends may tenderly fade,
But in our hearts, their presence won't evade.
For friendships ebb and flow like a rhyme,
Never constant through the sands of time.

FROM THE PORCH ROCKER

THE JOY OF SHARING

In a world filled with wonder and delight,
Where friendships bloom in the sun so bright,
There lies a secret, simple and true,
That sharing with friends is what we must do.

What does it mean to share, you may ask?
It's about giving freely from our joyful task.
For when we share with friends who hold our hearts,
We show them that they're an essential part.

Cooperative play becomes a gentle art,
As friends unite with open minds and hearts.
They take turns and negotiate with grace,
Knowing it's not about winning any race.

Sometimes disappointment may come into play,
But sharing teaches us to find another way.
To cope with setbacks and turn them around,
Creating harmony on friendship's sacred ground.

Sharing leads to compromise and all things fair,
An important lesson we all must bear.
For in giving a little to those we hold dear,
We receive something precious, crystal clear.

The joy of sharing cannot be contained,
It spreads like sunshine after rain.
It brightens days and warms our souls,
Connecting us together, making us whole.

ALI LUCE

So let us cherish these lessons small,
And heed the voice within friendship's call.
Share your toys and treasures every day,
And watch the magic unfold along your way.

For in the act of sharing lies a secret true—
Friendship deepens, for me and for you.
Let generosity guide each step we take,
In this world of wonder that we all create.

ABOUT THE AUTHOR

Ali Luce grew up in Hopkinton, Massachusetts, and discovered a passion for poetry at a young age. Currently studying computer science with a minor in classics at the University of New Hampshire, Ali's writing explores themes of change, love, and the human experience.

Milton Keynes UK
Ingram Content Group UK Ltd.
UKHW032329080824
446595UK00002B/48